INTERPLANETARY RESEARCH ARCHIVES LIBRARY

EST. 2247 • PRESERVING HUMANITY'S JOURNEY ACROSS THE STARS

MAN FROM EARTH ARCHIVES

• RECORDED BY L.I.S.A. •

DATE DUE	BORROWER NAME	DATE BOOKED OUT
12 APR 3617	XY'RATH-7	02 APR 3617
03 NOV 3789	VEL-KORA	19 OCT 3789
28 JUL 3924	THAE'LIN	11 JUL 3924
19 SEP 4138	QORVEX-II	01 SEP 4138
?? ??? 4200	UNKNOWN USER	?? ??? 4200

IAL FORM 77B
REV. 2247-7N

PROPERTY OF
I.P.R.A.

L.I.S.A. — The Mars Archive

Written and created by Tinus Etsebeth.

www.tinusetsebeth.co.za

"Your coffee is ready, sir."

SPEAKS ALL OFFICIAL MARS LANGUAGES:
ENGLISH • SPANISH • JAPANESE • AFRIKAANS • CHINESE • ZULU • FRENCH • GERMAN • ITALIAN

GR-3GG Brewer™

GET GREGG.
HE'S POLITE, FRIENDLY, AND MAKES THE BEST
CAPPUCCINO ON MARS.

GR-3GG BREWER™
IS FRIENDLY AND HELPFUL.
BUILT-IN MUSIC PLAYER INCLUDED.

10% DISCOUNT

ONLY VALID AT
★ **MARS MALL** ★
SHOP 602 ★

L.I.S.A 44

LIGHT-INTEGRATED INTELLIGENT SYNTHETIC ASSISTANT

Ironing upgrade available

MARS 2187
Hey, Johannes- how's the Coffee...mmm?
It's great, thanks, Gregg... time for my second cup.
Beep Beep
chirp chirp glitch
No problem! Another one coming up.
Beep
Here's to retirement
chirp shirrrpsh glitch
LiSA!
Your bird is glitching again.
READY!
I SEE IT JOHANNES.
rrrpsh glitch

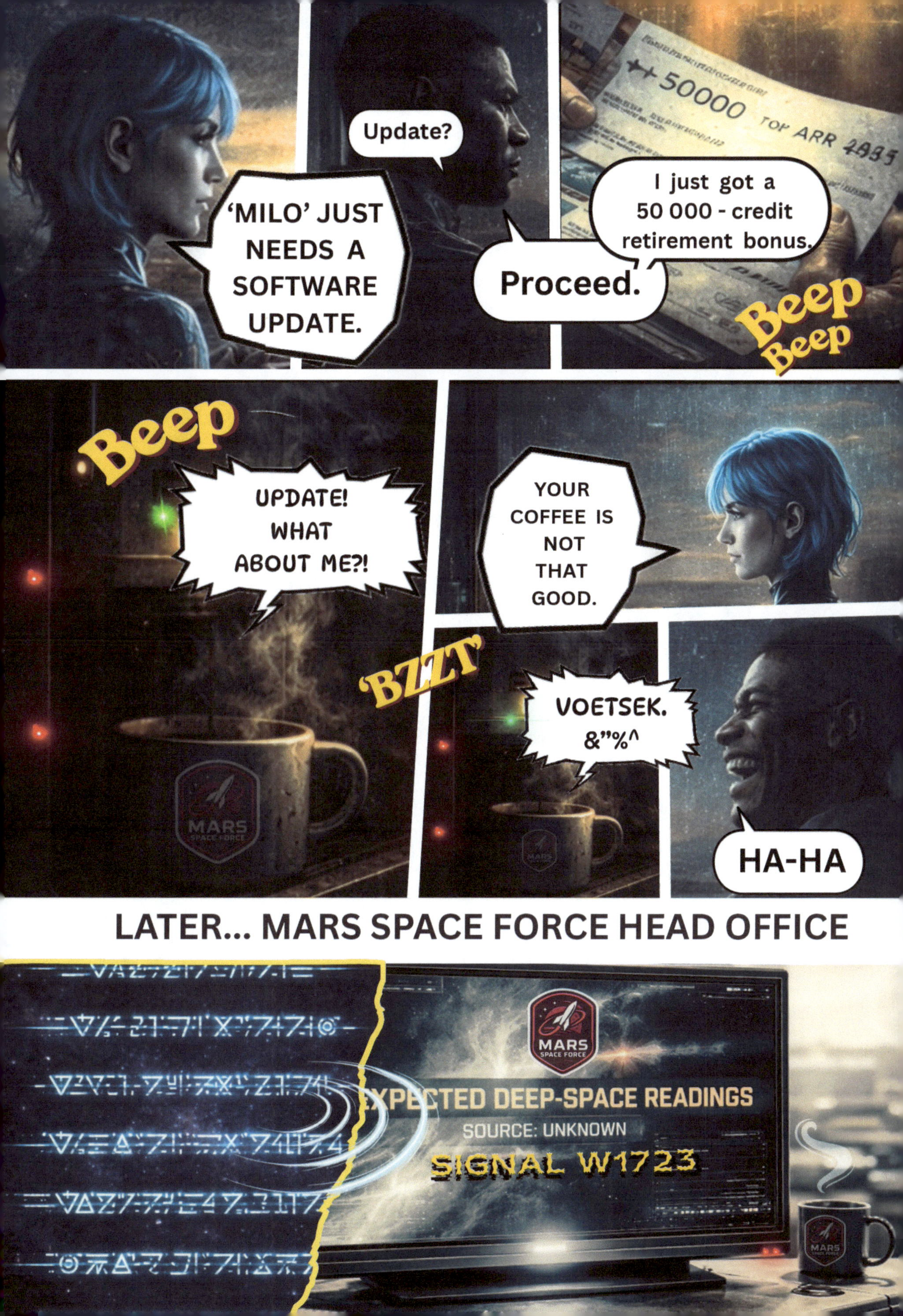

Beep

UPDATE! WHAT ABOUT ME?!

YOUR COFFEE IS NOT THAT GOOD.

'BZZT'

VOETSEK. &"%^

HA-HA

LATER... MARS SPACE FORCE HEAD OFFICE

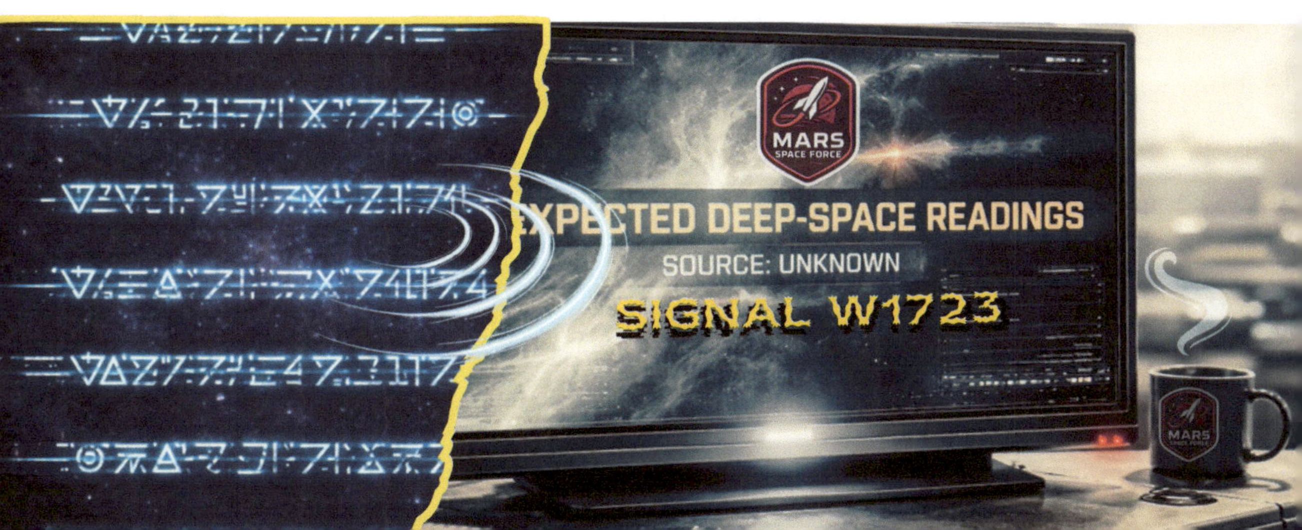

THIS IS MY FAVOURITE TELEVISION COMMERCIAL.
Click Click
We're out of milk.
Don't worry – I'll 'Get It Now™'.
VITAMIN MILK
VITAMIN
GET IT NOW
GET IT NOW™
MARS DELIVERY SERVICE
SIDE EFFECTS
IT'S A STUPID AD – IT DOESN'T EVEN LOOK LIKE MARS.
BZZT
MARS
SPACE FORCE

Later...
Ah... it started to rain.
RING RING
AAAGH— JOHANNES... YOUR SMALL HUMANS ARE CALLING.
RING
What?
YOUR GRANDCHILDREN ARE CALLING.
RING RING
JUPITER STATION
INCOMING CALL
Beep Beep
WARNING
UNEXPECTED DEEP-SPACE READINGS
SOURCE: UNKNOWN
Happy birthday, Tata!
I completely forgot.
YOU DON'T LOOK A DAY OLDER THAN YOU ARE.
Thank you, Lisa. I'm not sure if that was a compliment or sarcasm.
SARCASM!
BZZT
MARS
SPACE FORCE

Moments later...
IT IS BEAUTIFUL.
It was...
WAS? I DO NOT UNDERSTAND JOHANNES.
OH, YES.
Connecting to the server and downloading Earth's history.
CONFIRM TRANSFER
And book us a ticket to Cape Town...'ll explain later.
Beep
TO EARTH...?"
HEY, JOHANNES—WHAT ABOUT ME?
YOU'RE GOING TO NEED COFFEE.
It's been thirty years.
WHEN WAS THE LAST TIME YOU WERE THERE?
JOHANNES?
MARS
SPACE FORCE

VITAMIN
MILK
MAX-O_2
FORMULA

MAY CAUSE
UNFORESEEN
SIDE EFFECTS

GET IT NOW™
MARS DELIVERY SERVICE

IN 2 HOURS!

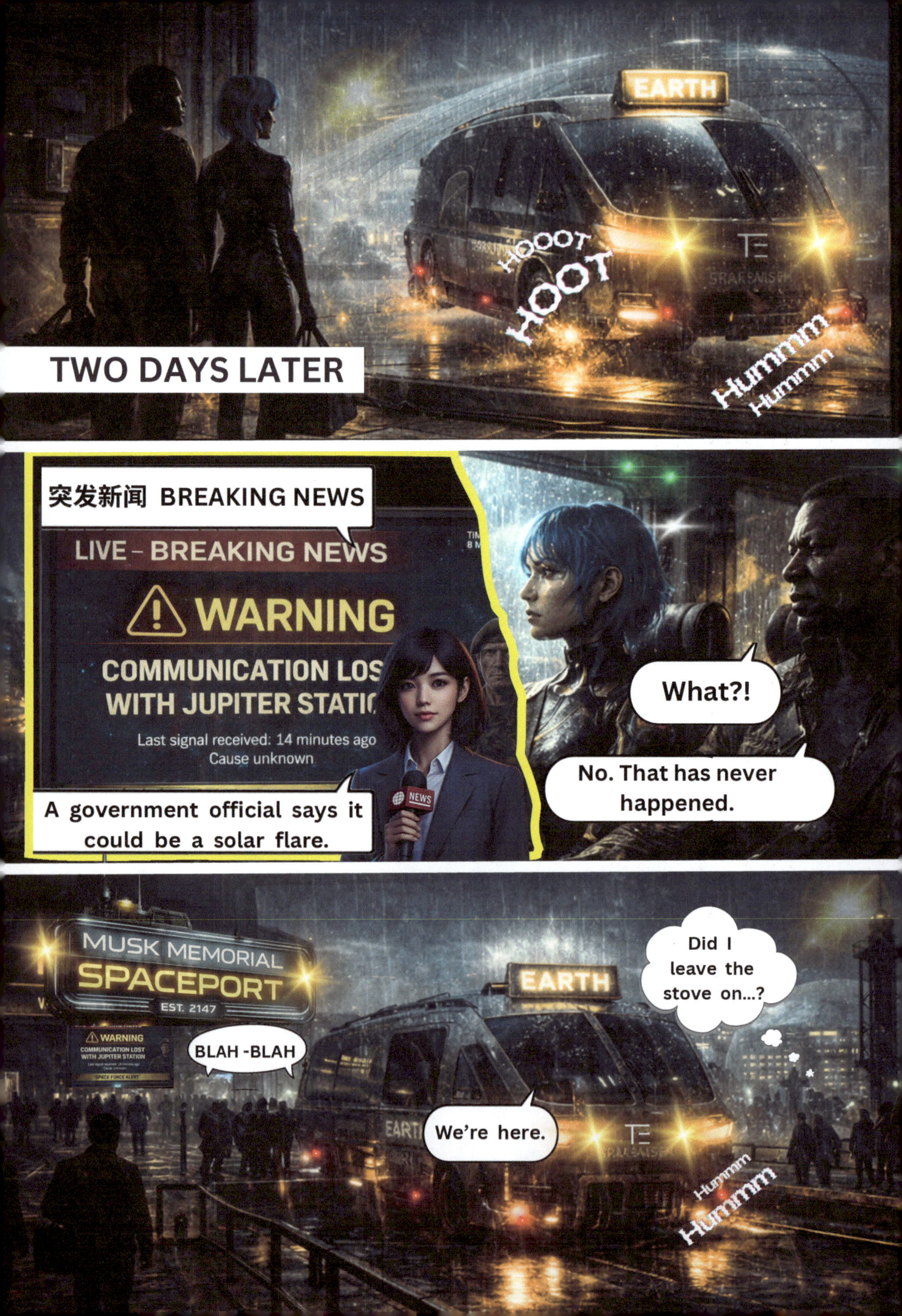

TWO DAYS LATER

EARTH
HOOOT
HOOT
Hummm
Hummm

SYSTEM CHECK... STANDBY
XR54TY
Trans Earth
FINAL NOTICE:
DEPARTING FOR EARTH IN 50 MINUTES.
Destination:
CAPE TOWN
DANGER: LOW O2
⚠ BRING ENOUGH O2 - EARTH WAYPOINT ⚠
CAPE TOWN CLOSED ⚠ until 2136
for fall out to clear. 24 hour gift shops.
YOUR BAG?
!
No, I'll keep the bag with me.
I AM SO EXCITED.
TICKETS! PLEASE
Go on ahead, Lisa.
I just need to say hello to an old friend.
Sawubona, Ricardo
Awe, ma se kind... Mbali.
WHERE CAN I GO FOR...
...?
2271

Is die bar al oop?
GOODBYE, MARS. SEE YOU SOON.
AUF WIEDERSEHEN, MARS.
XR54TY
SSSSHHHH
さようなら、火星。
WHOOOOOM
Johannes tells her what happened to Earth.
I'm sorry you had to find like this.
GALAXY GRAB
HUMANS DESTROYED EARTH.
SMILE!
Me and Johannes
TRANSPORT PA
ARRIVING AT EARTH IN 3 HOURS.
NUCLEAR FALLOUT DETECTED.
WARNING: LOW OXYGEN LEVELS DETECTED ON EARTH.
PUT ON YOUR MASKBEFORE EXITING.

Later...
EARTH 2187
Welcome to Earth.
We must take the shuttle from here.
CAPE TOWN
Castle of Good Hope

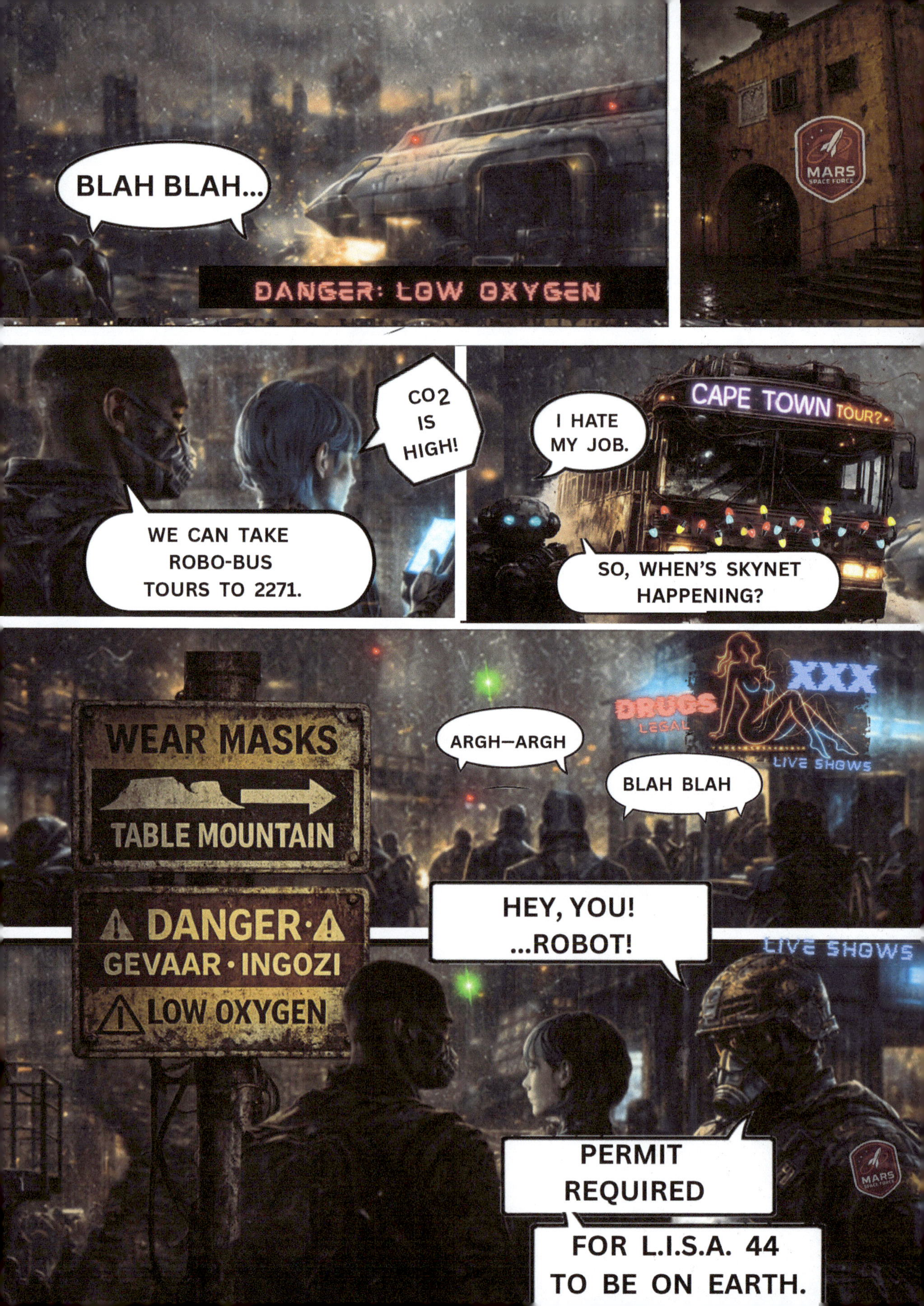

WEAR MASKS
TABLE MOUNTAIN
DRUGS
LEGAL
XXX
LIVE SHOWS
ARGH—ARGH
BLAH BLAH
DANGER
GEVAAR · INGOZI
LOW OXYGEN
HEY, YOU! ...ROBOT!
LIVE SHOWS
PERMIT REQUIRED
FOR L.I.S.A. 44 TO BE ON EARTH.

... ahh
Captain Mbali.
Sorry about that.
Rules are rules.
If you need any help, let...
ME.
Rookie.
AND...
I AM NOT A ROBOT.
HE REMINDS ME OF GREGG. YOUR STUPID COFFEE MACHINE.
WHAT ARE THEY DOING?
Surviving.
...Surviving.
YELLING
2271
BLAH BLAH
ARGH—ARGH
We're here.
WHERE?
2271
%^&!

VIVA!
YELLING
GALAXY GRAB
Welcome to 2271.
This is Earth's history you can touch—over 150 years old.
For music.
AMAZING
WHIRRR
BEEP
Rugby.
WHAT IS A... VIBRA—
Brrr
BRRR
EISH?!
EISH?!
Let's go.
Ready?
3...2...
Thank you
AMAZING. THANK YOU.

VIVA!
VIVA!
...1
Something isn't right.
Viva la resistance!
LISA!
WANTED
ELIAS RAX
REWARD: 150,000 CREDITS
CHARGES:
ZONE BREACH
SYSTEM SABOTAGE
IDENTITY UNREGISTERRED
LAST TRACKED: TABLE MOUNTAIN SAFE ZONE
PACE FORCE
UTHORITY
EVEL 4 THREAT
STATUS: HIGH RISK
SF-7782-CR
FILE PARTIALLY CORRUPTED
DO NOT
WHAT...
HAPPEND?

There are bad people out there.

MOVE!!

£$%&

The area is secure.
Go back to your homes and shops

FREE EARTH
FREE CAPE TOWN
LEAVE US ALONE
NO MORE MARS
ACE FORCE
DON'T NEED MARS

This isn't finished

Later...

LAST TRIP
FROM 18:20
TERRA NOVA
OXYNEL GENERATOR
NOT WORKING
WITHOUT SUN

One more thing I want to show you.

Then we leave Earth!

SCIENTISTS WARNED US FOR YEARS...

...for years. AND WE DID NOT LISTEN.

WORLD NEWS—2035

SCIENTISTS WARN:

TOO MANY PEOPLE

HUMAN RIGHTS TO BLAME?

One family. One child... rejected by the people.

WATER PRICE UP AGAIN

COUNTDOWN TO MARS

TERRAFORMING DEVICE ONLINE

ESCAPE NOT FOR EVERYONE

Everybody thought robots would end the Earth... especially that *XW7q4* robot.

I DON'T UNDERSTAND...

YOU DIDN'T LISTEN TO THE SMARTEST PEOPLE ON THE PLANET?!

The cable car is late!
IT'S NEVER LATE.
We didn't mean to ignore them.
We're only human...
YOU ARE ONLY HUMAN?
That was always the excuse...
Time to go.
RAX...— ACTIVATING IT NOW!
No! Don't— not yet!
Not here! You fool!
CLICK
WHAT ARE THOSE HUMANS DOING?
CLICK
WANTED
ELIAS RAX
DEAD
150,000 CREDITS
SAFE ZONE
SPACE FORCE AUTHORITY
There goes our lift...
We won't make it down in time.
The fallout cloud is almost here.
THE WAITING ROOM HAS EMERGENCY OXYGEN.

BREATHABLE AIR: DECLINING
TIME TO ZERO.
40 m
WAITING ROOM
EMPTY.
CH 126 LIVE
This is bad.
WARNING
DEADLY NUCLEAR FALLOUT
Meanwhile,
HURRY...!
BOMB SHELTER
ACCESS POINT
BLAH,BLAH
down the mountain...
OXYGEN: : 14%
EST. TIME: 38 m
So, This is Earth.
OXYGEN: : 14%
EST. TIME
IT'S STILL BETTER THAN GREGG'S COFFEE!.
LS-44
Ha-Ha

38 MINUTES LATER...
THANK YOU FOR SHOWING ME YOUR WORLD, JOHANNES.
Goodb...
Me and Johannes

THIS IS YOU

JOIN TODAY

+3M23 (432) 1345 2882

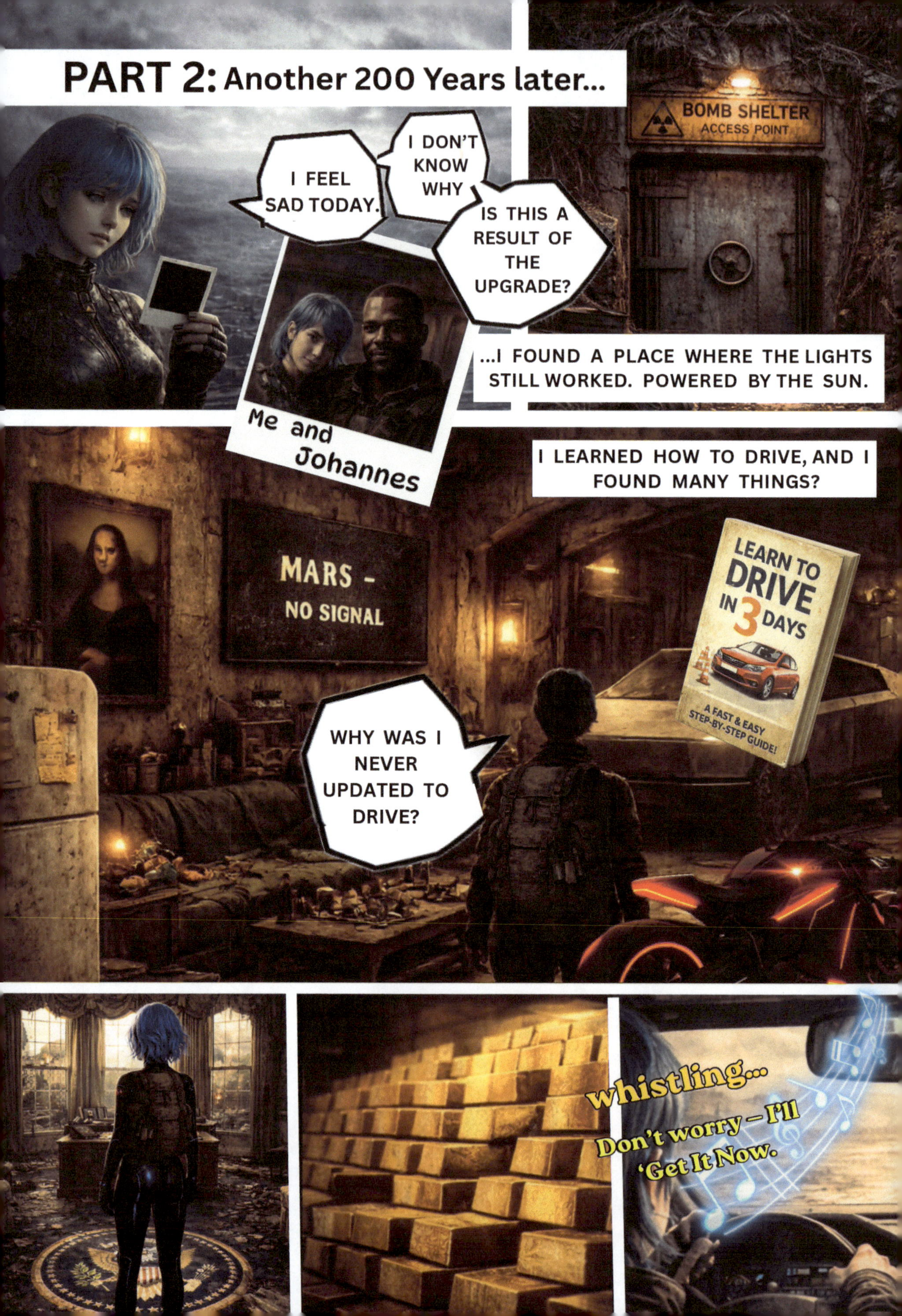

PART 2: Another 200 Years later...

I FEEL SAD TODAY.

I DON'T KNOW WHY

IS THIS A RESULT OF THE UPGRADE?

BOMB SHELTER
ACCESS POINT

Me and Johannes

...I FOUND A PLACE WHERE THE LIGHTS STILL WORKED. POWERED BY THE SUN.

I LEARNED HOW TO DRIVE, AND I FOUND MANY THINGS?

MARS -
NO SIGNAL

LEARN TO DRIVE IN 3 DAYS
A FAST & EASY STEP-BY-STEP GUIDE!

WHY WAS I NEVER UPDATED TO DRIVE?

JOHANNES...I DROVE INTO THE DESERT.
AND...
I FOUND SOMETHING WONDERFUL.
I DROVE FOR DAYS... WEEKS... YEARS—
FIRST, I FOUND A GREEN PLANT.
THEN, A FAMILY PICTURE. THEY LOOKED HAPPY.
WEEKS LATER
THEN THERE IT WAS... A CITY. WITH REAL HUMANS.
LAS VEGAS
WELCOME
FABULOUS
LAS VEGAS
NEVADA

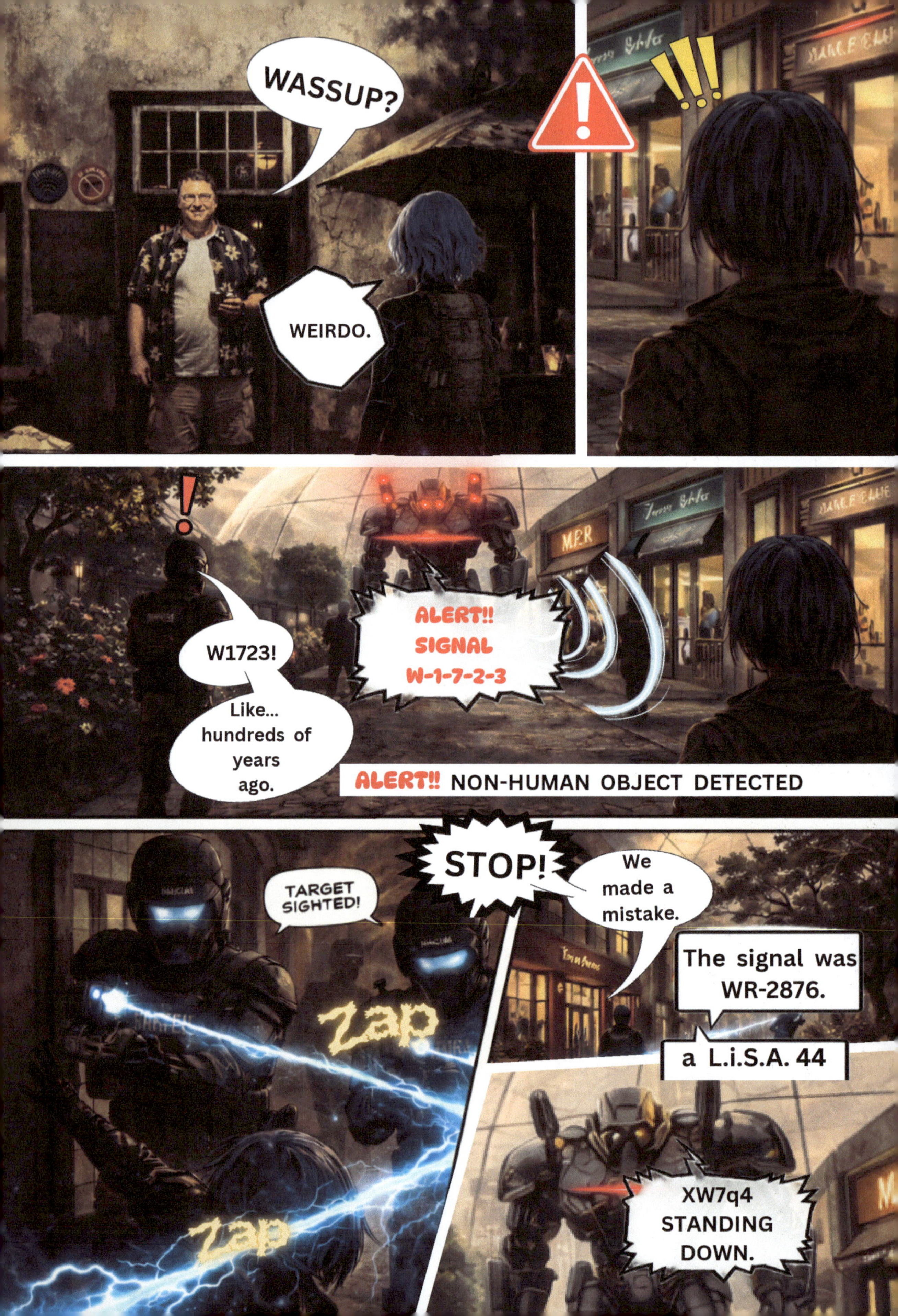

WASSUP?

WEIRDO.

TARGET SIGHTED!

STOP!

Zap

Zap

We made a mistake.

The signal was WR-2876.

a L.i.S.A. 44

XW7q4 STANDING DOWN.

LAS VEGAS

Searching for L.I.S.A.-44...

ACTIVE SCAN: L.I.S.A.-44

SCANNING

SCANNING

PART: 3 200 Years later...

AFTER SIX HUNDRED YEARS, THE EARTH IS CHANGING.

HAPPY BIRTHDAY, JOHANNES. 600 today.
I FOUND SOMETHING YESTERDAY.
WHY ARE YOU FOLLOWING ME?
WOOF WOOF
HOW RUDE.
IT BARKED AT ME.
WOEF
J M
BOOOOOOM
Moments later...
??
?
...WHAT WAS THAT?
GRR...
J M

2787
HUUUUUUUM
HUUUUUUUM
DATA TRANSFER
J M
GRR—
WOOF!

DATA TRANSFER COMPLETE
HUUUUUUK
HUUUUUUK
DO YOU UNDERSTAND?
BZZT
YES... I UNDERSTAND NOW.
WE WILL GO WITH YOU.
?
I HAVE BEEN ON EARTH FOR SIX HUNDRED YEARS.
J M
NO. YOUR COUNTER LIMITS AT SIX HUNDRED.
1400 YEARS?!
3587
HA-HA
BZZT
THE YEAR IS 3587 ...YOUR STAR CALCULATION.
Just saying.
BZZT
GREGG - I KNEW YOU WERE IN THE BACKPACK THE WHOLE TIME.
VOETSEK. %&£"
MARS SPACE FORCE

3587
THE REASON THEY CAME TO EARTH.
THE SIGNAL
SIGNAL DETECTED: IMPOSSIBLE. NO PRIOR ANALOGUE EXISTS.
SIGNAL W1723
IN 2187.
LATER
ACCESSING - L.I.S.A...
FILE INDEX INITIALISING...
PLANETARY RECORDS
!
MARS
MARS DESTROYED
ACCORDING TO YOUR HISTORICAL DATA, THIS PLANET WAS DESIGNATED: MARS.
L.I.S.A... WHAT DO YOU REMEMBER?

LISA ... WHAT DO YOU REMEMBER?

SPACE FORCE

1200 YEARS AGO...

SIGNAL

W-1-7-2-3.

SPACE FORCE

MARS
SPACE FORCE

CONTACT: 20 SPACECRAFT APPROACHING
ANOMALY BETWEEN MARS AND JUPITER

...14 Minutes Later

MARS
NO SIGNAL

MOONBASE 11

突发新闻 BREAKING NEWS

LIVE – BREAKING NEWS

WARNING

COMMUNICATION LOST
WITH JUPITER STATION

Last signal received: 14 minutes ago
Cause unknown

*SPACE FORCE ALERT

A government official says it could be a solar flare.

NEWS

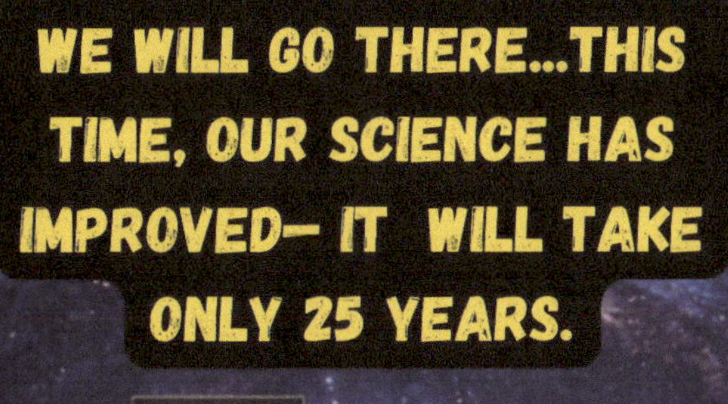

EARTH

WE TOOK SOME ITEMS WE FOUND ABANDONED FROM YOUR PLANET.

WE ARE FROM HERE.

LARRATA

WHAT IS THAT DELICIOUS SMELL?

COFFEE!

IT'S A LONG TRIP AHEAD. I HAVE COFFEE PLANT SEEDS.

Whirr

I THINK I NEED AN UPGRADE.

Beep

MARS SPACE FORCE

ONE YEAR LATER...
COFFEE RULES
WE LOVE COFFEE
01 COFFEE FIRST.
02 OXYGEN SECOND.
03 RESPECT THE BEAN.
GREGG
THANKS FOR UPGRADE.
COFFEE RULES
WE LOVE COFFEE
01 COFFEE FIRST.
02 OXYGEN SECOND.
03 RESPECT THE BEAN.
★ BY ORDER OF GREGG ★
DELICIOUS.
Beep
GREGG
TOLD YOU.
Whirr
...AND THANKS FOR THE UPGRADE.
100%
DECK 12
COFFEE PLANTATION

PART 4: 24 Years later.

3612

LARRATA MAGNA

WELCOME TO OUR PLANET.

COFFEE, ANYONE?

NO.

%$&* VOETSEK.

Bzzzszt

FROM HERE, WE WILL SEARCH FOR SIGNAL W-1-7-2-3.

WE HAVE DETECTED SIGNAL W-1-7-2-3 !

"TO BE CONTINUED"

L.I.S.A.

- MARS ARCHIVES -

THE SIGNAL W-1723

#2

2027

L.I.S.A

ISSUE #2

ETSEBETH COMICS

LS-44

ETSEBETH COMICS  www.tinusetsebeth.co.za

www.ingramcontent.com/pod-product-compliance
Lightning Source LLC
LaVergne TN
LVHW070158110826
845147LV00002B/440

* 9 7 8 1 0 6 7 2 0 3 7 1 9 *